OTTER
Goes to School

SAM GARTON

BALZER + BRAY

An Imprint of HarperCollinsPublishers

The artist used Adobe Photoshop to create the digital illustrations for this book.
Typography by Dana Fritts
16 17 18 19 20   SCP   10 9 8 7 6 5 4 3 2 1
❖
First Edition

To Mum and Dad, who taught me
(most of) everything I know

One morning, I asked Otter Keeper how he got to be so clever in the first place.

He told us that when he was little he went
to a super-fun place called school. At school
you learn a lot and get really clever.

School is why Otter Keeper is good at so many things and why he hardly ever makes spelling mistakes.

I decided I would start my own school! I knew a lot of people who weren't as clever as they could be.

After Otter Keeper left for work,
I got everyone ready.

We had to hurry.

Nobody wanted to be late on our first day.

At school I made sure everyone was settled in,
and then I said good-bye. This part was a bit sad.

I hoped the new teacher would look after everybody.

Luckily, just then,
the best teacher ever
arrived!

I apologized for being late and introduced myself to the class.

I showed them my special teacher dress

and my beautiful teacher purse

and, most important, my friendly
teacher face! Then I told everyone to
stop talking. It was time for school.

First it was time for math.
I wrote down all the numbers I knew.

No one could work out what to do after that.
So everyone just took turns holding the calculator.

Giraffe was very good at math.

I was very pleased with Giraffe.
I gave him lots of gold stars.

Next we had **music** lessons.

Pig had a beautiful singing voice.

I was very pleased with Pig.
I gave him several gold stars too.

After that it was story time.
I read everyone my favorite book.

I even did the different voices.

I was very pleased with me. So
I gave me the rest of the gold stars.

At lunch everyone was excited.
We were all feeling really clever!

Giraffe counted potato chips.

And Pig made up a funny song
all about lunch.

But Teddy was feeling sad.

I took Teddy aside for a friendly chat. He said he didn't like school. The other students were better than him at everything.

I had no idea what to do.

So I waited for Otter Keeper to come home.

As soon as he got back, we held an emergency
parent-teacher meeting at the big table.

I explained that Teddy wasn't good at

anything!

And that I wasn't very
good at being a teacher.

Otter Keeper gave me a cuddle. He said that everyone is good at something, and that you just need to find out what that something is. I think Otter Keeper is right.

There was time for one more lesson before dinner.

So we decided to have **art** class!

And when it was time to show our pictures,
something really wonderful happened. . . .

I showed everyone my picture of a tree.

Pig showed everyone his picture of a guitar.

Giraffe showed everyone his picture of a calculator.

And then Otter Keeper showed us
the picture Teddy had drawn all
by himself.

It was the best picture ever!

It turns out that Teddy was very good at art . . . and I was good at being a teacher after all!